BUG Z

ANN WEIL

ILLUSTRATED BY MICHAEL CHESWORTH

STECK-VAUGHN
ELEMENTARY · SECONDARY · ADULT · LIBRARY

A Harcourt Company

www.stec'

Cover illustration by Elizabeth Buttler

ISBN 0-7398-5137-3

Copyright © 2003 Steck-Vaughn Company

Power Up! Building Reading Strength is a trademark of
Steck-Vaughn Company.

Printed in China.

7 8 9 788 07

CONTENTS

CHAPTER ONE

THE BUG IN THE BOTTLE

Roberto struggled with three bags of recyclables. This was supposed to be his older sister Carmen's job, but she was on a date. Now he was stuck taking his family's empty bottles and cans down to the basement of the apartment building.

He opened the bin for glass. Something inside glistened. One of the bottles was glowing! Roberto picked it up. A big, weird bug was stuck inside.

It was larger than a cockroach and it had a bright blue body. There was a strange shape on its back that looked like the letter Z. The Z was blinking red.

What a cool bug! Roberto thought. He had been studying bugs since he was a little kid, but he had never seen this kind in any insect book.

Roberto took the bottle into the laundry room and held it upside-down over the sink. The bug slid out and fell into the basin.

Roberto put his hand next to the bug. The bug was half as big as his palm. Its antennae were twice as long as its body. They had little suction cups at the ends.

The bug touched Roberto's skin with one of its suction cups. Then it crawled onto his hand. The Z shape on the bug's back stopped flashing. It faded from red to orange to yellow.

Roberto slipped the bug into his pocket. It didn't try to crawl out. He finished sorting the recyclables quickly. Then he took the elevator back up to his floor.

"Grandma! Look what I found!" Roberto yelled, as he ran into the apartment.

"That's nice, dear," his grandmother said. She was pouring a glass of water and didn't look up when he came into the kitchen.

"But you haven't seen it yet!" Roberto protested.

"You always find the most interesting things." Mrs. Martinez wiped her hands on a towel. "Did you finish your homework?"

"Wake up, Roberto!"

Roberto opened his eyes to find Carmen kicking the side of his bed.

"Breakfast is ready," she said.

"Okay, I'm coming." Roberto hoped Carmen wouldn't notice the bug on his dresser. He had put it in a jar with holes in the lid.

"What's this?" Carmen asked. Roberto jumped out of bed.

"Grandma!" Carmen shrieked. "Roberto has a BUG!"

"A what, dear?" Mrs. Martinez asked from the kitchen.

"A dirty, ugly bug." Carmen looked sick.

"You can tell me all about it at breakfast," Mrs. Martinez called. "Your eggs are getting cold."

"That's disgusting!" Carmen snapped at Roberto, as she left his room.

Roberto put the jar in his backpack. He'd take the bug to school. Maybe his teacher could identify it.

Leo was in the elevator when it stopped on Roberto's floor. Roberto and Leo used to spend a lot of time together until last year. That's when Leo made the basketball team. Now, Leo always hung out with the other players. He didn't seem to have time for Roberto anymore. Roberto wished things were different.

"Leo! Look what I found in the basement!" Roberto pulled the bug jar out of his backpack.

"Later," Leo said, without even looking at it. "I'm late for practice." When the elevator door opened, Leo jogged away.

"I've never seen anything like this bug!" Roberto's teacher said. "You could use it for your Science Fair project. By the way, your partner is—" She looked at her notes. "Leo."

Roberto couldn't believe his bad luck. When he and Leo were little, Leo would cry whenever he saw a cockroach.

This project will be a disaster, Roberto thought. "Leo can't be my partner," he blurted out. "He's afraid of bugs!"

Leo groaned.

The teacher said, "I expect you two to work together, no excuses."

The bell rang, and Leo jumped out of his seat. He gave Roberto a mean look as he passed. Roberto hadn't meant to tell Leo's secret. He just wanted his project to be the best. Now he wished he'd kept quiet.

CHAPTER TWO

ONE OF A KIND

"Do you like your new home?" Roberto asked the bug. He had taken an old glass fish tank and covered the bottom with dirt. Then he put some rocks and twigs on top of the dirt so the bug would have something to climb on.

He had called Leo to ask him to come over and help, but Leo's mother had answered the phone. She told Roberto that Leo was out with friends from the basketball team. Roberto had left a message for Leo to call him as soon as he got back, but that was three hours ago.

Roberto placed a jar lid filled with water inside the tank. He covered the top of the tank with a piece of screen so the bug wouldn't be able to crawl out.

"Are you hungry? Do you like tuna?" Roberto tore off a piece of his tuna sandwich and put it inside the tank. The bug didn't move.

"I guess not," Roberto said. He wasn't sure what to feed the bug.

"I think I'll call you BugZ because you have a Z on your back," Roberto said. He made a little sign that said "BugZ" and taped it to the side of the tank.

"Roberto!" Carmen yelled. "Telephone. It's Leo."

Roberto made sure the screen lid was on tightly and went out to the hall phone. He hoped Leo wasn't still mad at him for telling the whole class he was afraid of bugs.

"Hi, Leo. What's up?" Roberto said.

"You called me, remember?" Leo said.

"I built a terrarium for BugZ," Roberto began.

"Bug-Zee?" Leo repeated.

"You know, the bug. I named it BugZ," Roberto explained.

"Whatever." Leo sounded bored.

"BugZ is really cool," Roberto argued. "It's not like other bugs. It's got this Z on its back that changes color and flashes."

"A bug is a bug," Leo said.

"Are you going to help me with this project or not?" Roberto demanded.

"I guess so. I don't really have a choice," Leo said.

"Okay, meet me on the elevator. We're going down to the basement to look for more bugs like BugZ." Roberto hung up before Leo could change his mind.

Roberto showed Leo the bin where he'd found BugZ.

"That's trash, man. I'm not touching that. Those bins are probably full of cockroaches." Leo stood back near the door.

Roberto picked through the bottles. There were no cockroaches. But there was nothing that looked like BugZ, either.

Suddenly, the door to the recycling room swung open.

"Hey, watch it!" Leo yelled. He rubbed his arm where the door had hit him.

Roberto turned and saw a strange-looking man in the doorway. He was wearing red plaid pants that were two inches too short and a blue and green striped shirt. A pair of thick glasses rested on the tip of his nose.

"I am so very sorry, young man," he said with an unusual accent. "I did not realize that anyone was here. I am Kelly. I am the new superintendent for this building. I was just . . . looking for something that I have lost. Perhaps you have seen it."

"There's nothing in here but trash and bugs," Leo said.

"Bugs?" Kelly took off his glasses. His eyes were a weird color. "Did you say *bugs?*"

"Yes, we're looking for—" Leo began.

Roberto elbowed him and said, "We're, uh, looking for a special bottle. Uh, my sister's favorite bottle. I accidentally threw it away and I thought it might still be in one of these bins."

"What are you talking about?" Leo said. "We're not looking for bottles. We're looking for bugs."

"Bugs? I am myself very interested in bugs," Kelly said. "Exactly what type of bug are you looking for?"

"Nothing," Roberto said. "Come on, Leo. I think my sister's bottle is still upstairs in the kitchen. Let's go, now!" Roberto grabbed Leo's sleeve.

"Easy on the clothes." Leo shook Roberto's hand away.

"Goodbye," said Kelly. "It was a pleasure to meet such fine young men as yourselves. Please feel free to come down another time, especially if you would like to discuss bugs."

"That man is strange," Leo said as they rode up in the elevator.

"Definitely," Roberto agreed.

"But why did you lie to him?" Leo asked.

Roberto shrugged. He wasn't sure why he didn't want to talk about BugZ with the new superintendent. Maybe Kelly had seemed too interested in bugs. "I think we should keep BugZ a secret, at least until we find out more about it," he said.

"Why?" Leo asked. "It's just a bug."

Roberto wasn't so sure about that.

CHAPTER THREE

◎

UNDERSTANDING BugZ

That evening after dinner, Leo helped Roberto move the terrarium from the floor onto a table next to the bedroom window.

"Why are we doing this?" Leo asked.

"I thought BugZ might enjoy looking out the window," Roberto answered.

Leo shook his head. "You're crazy, man," he said. "It's just a bug."

"Don't keep saying that!" Roberto argued. "BugZ is a special bug and deserves special treatment."

"What's so special about it?" Leo asked.

"I checked the school library," Roberto answered. "It's not in any of the bug books."

"So what?" Leo tapped the side of the terrarium. BugZ crawled to the side of the tank. The little suction cups on the ends of its antennae waved at Leo.

"See? It's saying hello," Roberto said.

"You're nuts," Leo said, but he smiled at BugZ.

Roberto took out his science notebook. "We have to figure out our Science Fair project."

"What, this isn't enough?" Leo gestured at the terrarium. BugZ was trying to climb up the side of the tank, but it kept slipping on the glass. The Z on its back turned from yellow to orange.

"I think BugZ is getting upset," Roberto said.

"So you're a bug mind reader now," Leo joked.

"Just watch the Z on its back. When it changes color from yellow to orange to red, it means something's bothering the bug," Roberto explained. "It was flashing red when BugZ was stuck in the bottle, but usually it's yellow."

"Let's try to get it to change color now," Leo suggested.

Roberto removed the screen top and put his hand inside the tank. BugZ crawled onto his palm. The Z on its back faded from orange to yellow.

"I've got an idea," Roberto said. "Our project can be about how and why the Z changes color. We can make a big chart showing the different colors and what they mean."

Leo nodded. "Sounds good."

"It's not good. It's GREAT!" said Roberto. "Our project will win first prize at the Science Fair!"

"What's that noise?" Leo asked. "It sounds like snoring."

"BugZ makes that sound when it's happy, sort of like a cat purring." Roberto gently stroked BugZ's back with one finger. The buzzing sound grew louder. "Here, do you want to hold it?"

Roberto held out his hand. BugZ looked up at Leo and waved its antennae.

"No way, man!" Leo cried, stepping back. "Keep that ugly thing away from me."

"You're not really afraid of BugZ, are you?" Roberto asked.

Leo didn't answer Roberto's question. Instead, he said, "I thought you said we had work to do. Let's get it over with so I can go practice."

"Well, the first thing is to figure out what BugZ likes to eat," Roberto said. "I saved bits of my dinner and put them in the tank. But the food is all still there. BugZ wouldn't eat any of my tuna sandwich, either."

"Maybe it likes candy," Leo suggested. He took a roll of hard candies out of his pocket and popped a red one into the tank.

BugZ crawled over to the piece of candy and picked it up with the suction cups on the ends of its antennae.

"See," Leo said with a smile. "I know what this bug likes."

BugZ dropped the candy and looked up at Roberto and Leo. The Z on its back went from yellow to green.

"I don't think BugZ likes the candy," Roberto said.

"What does green mean?" Leo asked.

"I don't know. I've only seen it turn from yellow to orange to red, then back to yellow."

"Now it's turning blue." Leo suddenly sounded worried. "That bug looks sick."

The Z on BugZ's back was almost invisible against its blue body.

"I think it's hungry," Roberto said.

"So what are we supposed to do?" Leo asked.

Roberto felt a lump form in his throat. He said, "We'd better find something it likes to eat soon, or BugZ's going to starve to death!"

CHAPTER FOUR

THE SECRET LABORATORY

Leo logged on to the Internet using the computer in Roberto's living room. Roberto looked over his shoulder.

"There are hundreds of bug sites," Leo said. "I can't believe so many people are into bugs."

"There's a bug chat room," Roberto said. "Maybe someone online will know what BugZ likes to eat."

Leo typed: "Does anyone know anything about a bug with a Z on its back? What does it eat?"

"What if no one answers us?" Roberto glanced over at the terrarium. BugZ hadn't moved for more than an hour. Its Z had disappeared and its antennae were limp.

"Look!" Leo yelled.

A reply to their question flashed onto the screen: "I know of such a bug. This bug eats rotten vegetables."

"All right!" Roberto pumped his fist in the air. "Let's get BugZ something to eat."

Leo logged off, and the two boys went to the refrigerator. There was some old lettuce in the bottom of the vegetable drawer. Roberto took an outside leaf that was brown around the edges and put it in the terrarium next to BugZ.

"Please, BugZ, eat," Roberto begged.

One of the suction cups moved toward the lettuce, then the other. The bug lifted the lettuce leaf. BugZ was eating!

Just then, the doorbell rang. Roberto heard Carmen ask who it was and then open the door.

"Roberto!" Carmen yelled. "The superintendent needs to check your room. There's a leak upstairs, and he wants to see if there's water damage in our apartment."

"Just a minute," Roberto yelled. He whispered to Leo, "We've got to hide BugZ!"

"Why?" Leo asked.

"I don't want Kelly to see it," Roberto explained.

"You're paranoid," Leo said, but he threw a blanket over BugZ's terrarium.

"What are you doing, Leo? BugZ won't be able to breathe. I want to hide it, not kill it." Roberto was just taking off the blanket when the door to his room opened. Carmen and the superintendent stepped in.

"Hello, young men," Kelly said. "It is a pleasure to see you both again."

"Uh, hi," Roberto said. He jumped in front of the terrarium to hide it from view.

"And what is that behind you?" Kelly asked. He tried to look over and around Roberto. Each time Kelly moved, Roberto moved to block his view.

"Oh, that's just my brother's bug," Carmen answered for Roberto.

"A bug? How interesting. May I please see your bug?" Kelly asked Roberto.

"What's the big deal about a bug?" Leo replied. "If you've seen one, you've seen them all."

"Not at all, young man. Bugs can be as different from each other as you and I," Kelly said. "Where I come from, bugs are honored and respected."

"And where exactly are you from?" Roberto asked. Something about Kelly seemed very suspicious.

But the superintendent didn't answer Roberto's question. He moved closer to the terrarium to try to get a better look at BugZ.

"Didn't you say you were looking for water damage?" Leo asked as he stepped in front of Kelly. "I don't see any here. Maybe you should look somewhere else."

BANG! A sudden loud noise from the street startled them.

"What's that?" Kelly asked.

As the boys and Carmen ran to look out the window, Kelly poured a thick, green liquid into BugZ's water.

"It must have been a truck backfiring," Leo said.

"What is that smell?" Carmen asked. She looked at Roberto as if the smell were coming from him.

"It's not me," Roberto said. "It's coming from BugZ's terrarium."

"It smells awful." Carmen wrinkled her nose in disgust.

"I must be going now," Kelly said. As he walked past BugZ's tank, he leaned in and whispered, "I will be back for you!"

"Did you say something?" Roberto asked.

"I said, 'Goodbye, my new friends.'"

After Kelly and Carmen had left, Leo said, "I think Kelly put something in BugZ's tank when we were looking out the window."

"Well, if he did, BugZ liked it," Roberto said. "Look!"

The Z on BugZ's back was glowing a healthy yellow.

"This is boring," Leo said. He and Roberto were sitting in the laundry room. They were pretending to wait for their clothes to dry, but they were really spying on Kelly. They noticed he spent a lot of time in a broom closet next to the laundry room.

"What do you think is in there?" Leo asked.

Roberto shrugged. "I don't know, but I'd like to find out."

They waited until Kelly left, then they tried the door.

"It's locked," Roberto said, disappointed.

"No, it's just stuck." Leo kicked the door open with his foot. It was dark inside. "Where's the light?" he asked.

Roberto felt around for a switch and knocked something off a shelf. It crashed to the floor.

"Don't trash the place," Leo said. He found the light switch and flicked it on.

That's when he saw the cockroaches. Dozens of them were crawling out of the box that Roberto had knocked off the shelf.

"Oh no," Roberto said softly. "Leo, don't—"

But Leo had already run out of the room.

Roberto was about to go after Leo when he saw that the closet was really a little laboratory. More boxes of cockroaches sat on one shelf. Each box had a plastic window so you could see inside. On another shelf, Roberto saw several bottles filled with colored liquids.

Then Roberto saw a small computer. He looked more closely.

This looks like Kelly's e-mail, he thought. He read a few of the sent messages. One was about washing machines. Another was about soap. Then, Roberto read one that made him shiver:

"I will bring some Earth beings back with me. No one will notice that a few are missing. They might save our kind from dying out. I will leave as soon as I reclaim the bug."

Only someone from another planet would call people "Earth beings," Roberto thought. He felt his stomach tighten with fear. Kelly was an alien!

CHAPTER FIVE

THE SCIENCE FAIR

Roberto ran into the kitchen. "Grandma, the new superintendent is an alien!"

Mrs. Martinez was taking a batch of cookies out of the oven. "Well, dear, you know your Grandpa and I were considered aliens when we first arrived from Cuba. That was over forty years ago."

"Not that kind of alien, Grandma," Roberto said. "He's a real alien, from another planet. An extraterrestrial."

"Oh, I loved that movie *E.T.* That cute little thing reminded me of my first puppy. Would you like a cookie, dear?"

"Uh, no thanks." Roberto loved his grandmother, but sometimes he couldn't tell if she really listened to him.

But who else could help him? He couldn't ask Carmen. She wouldn't believe him. His teacher? She would just call his grandmother. They might think he was sick and make him miss the Science Fair, which was tomorrow.

That left Leo, who was already upset about the cockroaches. What would he do if he found out that Kelly was an evil alien planning to kidnap them?

Suddenly, Roberto realized what Kelly had meant by "reclaiming the bug." He was going to try to take BugZ, too! Roberto knew he had to do something. He dialed Leo's number. It rang four times. He was about to hang up when Leo answered the phone.

"Leo, it's Roberto. Listen, you've got to get over here right away!"

"Can't do it," Leo said. "I just got home from practice. I have to shower—"

Roberto cut him off. "There's no time. That new superintendent is...uh, he's a rare bug collector and he's trying to steal BugZ."

"Are you sure? How do you know that?" Leo asked.

"After you, uh, left that closet where Kelly was working, I looked around and found some papers," Roberto lied.

"Listen, I've had enough bugs for one day." Leo sounded tired. "I've got to go."

"Okay," Roberto said. "Let's get to school early tomorrow morning. I don't want to be late for the Science Fair—" But Leo had already hung up. Roberto went into his bedroom and lay down on his bed, feeling very scared and alone.

The Science Fair was held in the school cafeteria. The boys had brought BugZ's terrarium to school in an old wagon that once had belonged to Leo's little brother. They put the terrarium on one of the tables and taped a chart to the front of the table. The chart showed the colors of the Z and what each color meant.

The judges walked from table to table as students demonstrated their projects. Everyone from the school was walking around the cafeteria, looking at the different exhibits.

Suddenly, Roberto thought he saw a flash of red plaid in the crowd.

"I think I just saw Kelly," Roberto whispered to Leo.

Before Leo could say anything, the judges announced the winners of the Science Fair: "Roberto Martinez and Leo Ruiz!"

"We won!" Leo yelled, raising his fist in the air.

But Roberto wasn't so happy. He was worried. He scanned the crowded cafeteria, looking for Kelly.

One of the judges spoke into a microphone. "Roberto, Leo, would you come up here for a moment? We have prizes for you."

"Come on," Leo said. "Let's go."

"You go," Roberto said. "I'll wait here with BugZ."

"No way, man. You're coming with me. This was your idea." Leo pushed Roberto up to the front of the cafeteria where the judges were waiting for them. They each received a gift certificate for their local bookstore.

"I'm going to get a book about bugs," Leo said.

Roberto wasn't thinking about what book he would buy with his prize. When he was at the judge's table, he had seen Kelly again. Roberto ran back to their table and looked inside the terrarium. BugZ was gone!

CHAPTER SIX

HOME AT LAST

"Where's BugZ?" Leo asked.

"Kelly must have taken him!" Roberto guessed. "Come on, maybe we can still catch him!" The boys raced out of the cafeteria.

"Looking for this?"

Roberto stopped when he heard his grandmother's voice behind them. She was holding a jar with holes in the lid. Inside the jar was BugZ.

"How did you . . . what are you doing here?" Roberto asked.

Mrs. Martinez smiled. "I thought you might need a little extra help today. I arrived just as the judges announced you two had won. I was so proud of you. Then, I saw Kelly trying to steal BugZ while you were with the judges. He was putting BugZ in a jar. I knew you were suspicious of him. You're a smart boy, so I trusted your judgment about him. I sneaked up behind him, grabbed the jar, and ran."

Roberto hadn't realized his grandmother was so observant or that she had such faith in him.

"Wow." Roberto was impressed. "Thanks, Grandma!" He gave his grandmother a big hug.

Mrs. Martinez handed the jar to Leo so she could hug Roberto back. Leo noticed that the Z on BugZ's back was red. He opened the lid and let BugZ crawl out onto his hand.

"What are you doing?" Roberto asked, amazed. Leo was actually touching a bug.

"BugZ was upset." Leo gently stroked BugZ's back. BugZ seemed happy to be out of the jar and in Leo's hand. The Z on its back faded to a golden yellow.

"Listen, I've got something to tell you two." Roberto told his grandmother and Leo about the e-mail he had seen on Kelly's computer.

"Do you really think he's planning to kidnap humans?" Mrs. Martinez asked.

"I don't know," Roberto answered. "Maybe."

"Well, he's not getting this bug," Leo said.

"Come on, let's go home," Mrs. Martinez suggested. "We'll take care of this together."

Roberto wasn't sure how his grandmother planned to "take care" of an evil alien, but he was pretty sure she could do it.

Roberto kept glancing back over his shoulder as they walked home. He expected Kelly to jump out at them any moment. He tripped on the curb and bumped into Leo.

"Watch where you're going!" Leo said. "You almost made me drop BugZ."

"Sorry," Roberto apologized. "I was looking for—"

"Kelly!" Mrs. Martinez shouted, pointing ahead of them. The alien was on a bicycle, and he was pedaling in their direction.

"Uh-oh." Roberto bit his lip. They couldn't outrun someone on a bicycle.

Kelly was coming toward them so fast that he was almost a blur. He was less than a block away and he wasn't slowing down.

"How do you stop this thing?" Kelly yelled just before he crashed the bike into the side of a building right in front of them.

"That poor man! I hope he isn't hurt," Mrs. Martinez said.

"He's not a man," Roberto reminded his grandmother. "He's an alien, remember?"

Kelly stood up and brushed the dirt off his hands. "Good afternoon," he said. "I am sorry I do not have time for conversation. I must ask you to return my bug to me immediately."

"No way," said Leo, clutching BugZ's jar more tightly.

"Your bug?" Mrs. Martinez was confused.

"Kelly brought BugZ to Earth with him and now he's going back," Roberto guessed. "And he's going to kidnap us and take us with him!"

"Kidnap?" Now Kelly looked confused.

"Don't try to deny it," Roberto said to Kelly. "I read your e-mail about bringing Earth beings back with you."

"Ah, now I understand," Kelly said. "I had better tell you everything. You already know so much. It is true that I am from another planet. But I am a scientist, not a kidnapper. The Earth beings I referred to were cockroaches, not human beings."

"Cockroaches?" Leo said. "Take as many of those pests as you want. The fewer here on Earth, the better."

"I see you do not like bugs, my young friend.

But on my planet, bugs are well loved," Kelly explained. "Unfortunately, they are dying out. You see, my home planet has too many people living on it. There is not enough land to grow food anymore, so now we make and eat synthetic food. But our bugs do not like the synthetic food. They prefer rotten vegetables. That was what I put in BugZ's tank yesterday—liquid vegetables.

"Our bugs are not adapting to the changes on our planet. That is why I am here—to study your cockroaches. Cockroaches have survived millions of years on Earth because they have changed. Unless I find a way to help our dear bugs adapt, too, they will become extinct."

"That is so sad." Mrs. Martinez wiped a tear from her cheek.

Roberto wasn't moved. He wasn't going to give BugZ to Kelly. Even if BugZ was Kelly's bug, it sounded as though life here on Earth would be healthier for it. Besides, Roberto had grown to like the little guy.

Leo seemed to feel the same way as Roberto. "Why don't you just take all the cockroaches you want and leave BugZ here with us? We'll take good care of it."

"It'll get plenty of rotten vegetables," Roberto added.

"You do not understand," Kelly continued. "I have had this bug you call BugZ since I was born. I cannot leave without my bug."

"Maybe we should leave it up to BugZ," Leo suggested. He took BugZ out of the jar and held the bug in his hand. The Z on BugZ's back glowed a sunny yellow. "Hold out your hand," Leo instructed Kelly.

BugZ reached out its antennae to Kelly and touched his hand with its suction cups. But it didn't move from Leo's hand.

"What you say is true," Kelly said sadly. "My bug prefers to stay. Perhaps it knows it will be happier here."

BugZ waved its antennae at Kelly.

"Goodbye, my little friend," Kelly said. "And goodbye to you, my Earth friends." Then he turned and walked away.

"I hope the bugs on Kelly's planet will be okay," Mrs. Martinez said as they started walking toward home again.

Leo put BugZ back in the jar. "I think I'd like to keep BugZ at my apartment," Leo said.

"No way!" Roberto argued. "I found it, remember?"

"Why don't you share BugZ?" Mrs. Martinez suggested.

Leo and Roberto looked at each other. Then they both looked at BugZ. "Okay," they said together.

"Good. Leo, you can have BugZ this week, and next week, it's Roberto's turn," Mrs. Martinez said. The boys nodded.

Just then, one of Leo's friends passed them, dribbling a basketball. "Hey, Leo! Want to shoot a few?"

"Not now. I'm busy," Leo answered. Then he turned to Roberto. "Maybe we can stop at the grocery store and see if they have any rotten vegetables for BugZ."

Roberto smiled. Not only did he have BugZ, he also had his friend back.